Noticing

WRITTEN BY Kobi Yamada

ILLUSTRATED BY Elise Hurst

"*It's a beautiful day, isn't it?*"

It seemed as if someone was talking to me.
"It's okay, I guess," I replied.

"Just okay?" a woman sitting nearby responded.
"Why, we have the birds, the trees, the sky,
the questions, the what-ifs, and the why-nots!
I'd say this is indeed an exceptional day to
be alive. Don't you think?"

"If you say so," I shrugged. It seemed like
an ordinary day to me.

"Are you a painter?" I asked.

"I like to think of myself as more of a noticer really,"
she answered. "I just try to make things from what I
see. It is my way of appreciating and honoring them."

As I looked at her canvas, I couldn't believe what I was seeing. *How could someone create something so amazing?* I wondered. She was *definitely* a painter.

She looked over to me and asked, "When you look up, what do you see?"

"Clouds?"

"You see clouds? That's all? Just clouds?" the painter asked, astonished.

"I think so...," I said, uncertain, as I scanned the sky. "Why? What do you see?"

"Oh, so much!" she said excitedly. "It's like the whole sky is tempting me to be amazed. I see wild horses running free. And upside-down castles. I see whales flying like songbirds and a dragon breathing fire.

"But it's not only that. I'm filled with butterflies of excitement. It feels like an adventure is unfolding and I don't want to miss any of it!"

I stared up wanting to see what she saw.

"The more you pause and allow for the extraordinary,"
the painter explained, "the more you find it."

"And often what we see depends on what we look for.

"Take this mountain for instance." She gestured to the horizon.
"A climber might see a great challenge, a scientist might see the
movement of an ancient glacier, and someone else might notice
the cool breeze traveling from its snowy peaks. Though we all may
look at the same thing, we don't always see it in the same way.
That is true for mountains, and also for people."

"When we look at others, we may see their faces or their clothes," she continued. "But we are only seeing a tiny piece of who they really are. We often don't notice the important things, like their capacity for love, what they hope for, what they dream of, or who they can become.

"We can often miss the most beautiful parts of them."

I wondered what I wasn't noticing. I wondered what I was missing.

"What do you see in you?" asked the painter.

I looked down at my hands, my clothes, my shoes that were a size too big so I could grow into them. "Just a kid like any other kid, I suppose."

"But you are not like anyone else. In fact, there isn't another person exactly like you anywhere," the painter encouraged, "and the amazing thing is, there never has been and there never will be ever again."

"I'm not sure there is anything all that special about me," I said.

"Oh, but everything is special about you!
There really isn't a single thing about you that
isn't extraordinary," she shared enthusiastically.
"You are the rare and unique combination of what
was and the bright possibility of what can be."

"And you know what? So is everyone else.

"Everyone shines and needs to be seen. Everyone wants to know that they matter, that there is a place for them, and that they are needed. Sure, some may hide their brilliance, but the light is in there, always flickering, and it is a beautiful thing when we can reflect it back to them."

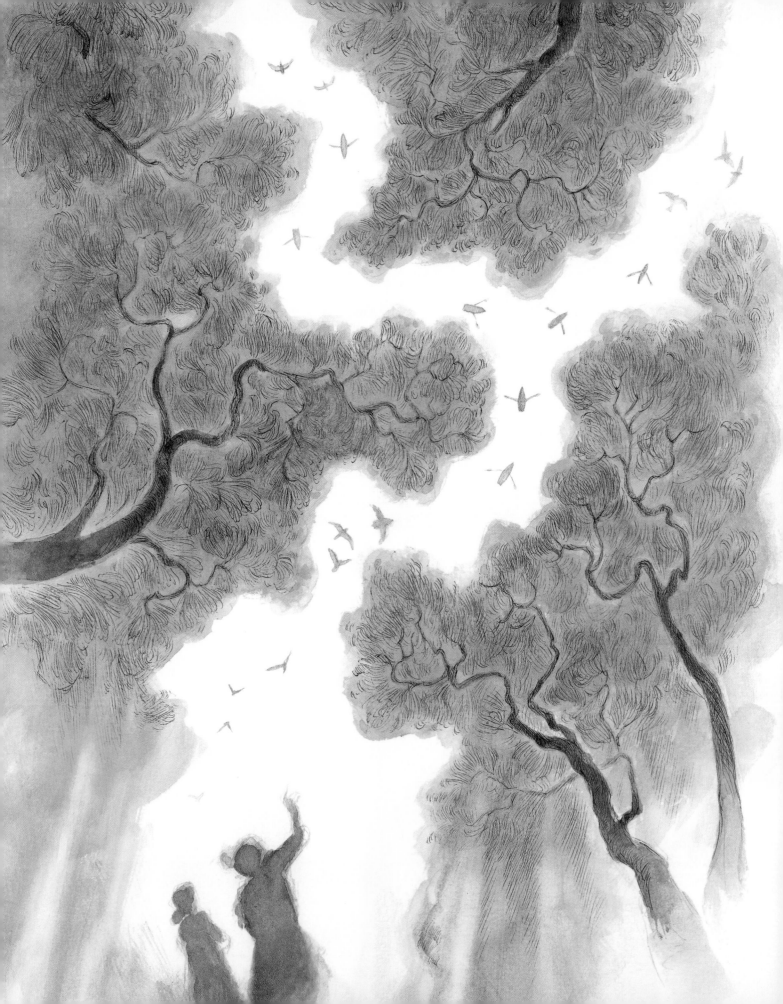

I always looked forward to my visits with the painter.
I had to admit, as much as I couldn't wait to see her,
I also couldn't wait to see what she saw.

On one occasion, I went to go find her and
she was sitting peacefully with her eyes shut.

"What are you doing?" I asked shyly,
not wanting to interrupt her.

"Hello, you." She smiled and waved me over.

"Some days I find that I can notice even more when I close my eyes," she explained. "The gentle rustling of my hair, the ideas dancing in my head, the sunshine on my face, and the wonder of being alive."

She invited me to close my eyes.

"What does home look like to you? What does kindness feel like? What does love look like?" the painter asked. "What does it feel like to have a friend? What does it look like to be one?

"One of the most important ways we see is with our imagination. So many significant things cannot be seen with your eyes, but they are very real. And it is vital that you look for and believe in them."

I was filled with a feeling of calm and appreciation. It was moving and wonderful. I sat there with my eyes closed, picturing the people and places and things that meant so much to me in my life.

"One of the best things you can be is interested," the painter shared. "When you are interested, you are curious, and when you are curious, you discover things—amazing things, about yourself and about the world."

"The miraculous is everywhere and in everything.
Waiting for us to notice it. Waiting for us to
appreciate it. Waiting for us to love it."

It's been years since that day when I first met the painter.
I miss her. I wish she were still here so I could tell her what
she has meant to me and how she helped me to look at
everything differently.

But mostly, what I wish I could say is, *thank you for seeing me.*

Dear Shale and Ever,
May you always be open
to the unbelievable beauty
around and within you.
Love,
Dad

For Kobi and all those
who see with their hearts.
EH

COMPENDIUM®
live inspired

Written by: Kobi Yamada
Illustrated by: Elise Hurst
Edited by: Amelia Riedler
Art Direction by: Jessica Phoenix

Library of Congress Control Number: 2022933412 | ISBN: 978-1-970147-89-6

1st printing. Printed in China with soy and metallic inks on FSC®-Mix certified paper. A012210001

*Create
meaningful
moments
with gifts
that inspire.*

CONNECT WITH US
live-inspired.com | sayhello@compendiuminc.com

  @compendiumliveinspired
#compendiumliveinspired